The Kingdom of Wrenly

15
Den of Wolves

By Jordan Quinn
Illustrated by Robert McPhillips

LITTLE SIMON

New York   London   Toronto   Sydney   New Delhi

LITTLE SIMON

An imprint of Simon & Schuster Children's Publishing Division
1230 Avenue of the Americas, New York, New York 10020
First Little Simon paperback edition June 2020
Copyright © 2020 by Simon & Schuster, Inc.
Also available in a Little Simon hardcover edition.
All rights reserved, including the right of reproduction in whole or in part in any form.
LITTLE SIMON is a registered trademark of Simon & Schuster, Inc., and associated colophon is a trademark of Simon & Schuster, Inc.
For information about special discounts for bulk purchases, please contact
Simon & Schuster Special Sales at 1-866-506-1949 or business@simonandschuster.com.
The Simon & Schuster Speakers Bureau can bring authors to your live event. For more information or to book an event contact the Simon & Schuster Speakers Bureau at 1-866-248-3049 or visit our website at www.simonspeakers.com.
Manufactured in the United States of America 0520 RR4
4 6 8 10 9 7 5 3
This book has been cataloged with the Library of Congress.
ISBN 978-1-5344-6526-8 (hc)
ISBN 978-1-5344-6525-1 (pbk)
ISBN 978-1-5344-6527-5 (eBook)

CONTENTS

CHAPTER 1

Mr. Mysterious

"I did it!" Clara exclaimed as she pounded the last stake into the ground with her mallet. "My tent is finally all set up!"

Prince Lucas groaned. "Stop bragging," he complained.

Poor Lucas had been struggling with his tent. He couldn't attach the canvas to the top of the center pole. It was too high.

Clara laughed and shook her head. Then she snapped her fingers, and Ruskin sat up. The scarlet dragon grabbed the prince's canvas in his teeth, flew it to the top of the pole, and secured it easily.

Lucas sighed and said, "Why didn't *I* think of that?"

"Perhaps you like a challenge," Clara suggested.

The prince frowned. "Not *that* kind of challenge. Besides, I thought camping was supposed to be fun."

Clara smirked. "I don't know . . . I'm having a great time watching the prince of Wrenly battle the dreaded tent monster."

"Ha-ha." Lucas gave a fake laugh. "Would you lend me a hand already?"

Clara helped the prince tighten the ropes and pound his stakes into the ground. They set up cots and chairs inside their tents.

"Now we can hike to Goblin Falls!" Lucas said triumphantly.

Lucas and Clara had never been to Goblin Falls before.

It was known to be the most magnificent waterfall in Wrenly. They had traveled across the bridge to the island of Burth to see it.

"My father says when you stand beside the falls, it's like standing on the edge of the world," said Lucas.

Clara tried to imagine it. "I've heard when the water crashes onto the rocks, the spray makes you feel as if you're floating on a cloud."

Somebody grunted behind them. It was Grom, one of the kingdom's smartest and sometimes grumpiest wizards. He had joined Lucas and Clara on their trip.

"Goblin Falls is nothing more than a lot of water falling off a cliff," the wizard said.

Lucas rolled his eyes. He didn't understand why Grom had wanted to come along. Grom didn't care about waterfalls, and he wasn't the type to sit beside a campfire and roast marshmallows, either. Grom liked to practice wizardry, and that was all.

"Would you like help with your tent?" the prince offered. "I've just learned the secret to hitching the canvas to the post."

Grom rolled up his sleeves.

"I can certainly handle putting up a tent, my prince," he said. Grom closed his eyes, splayed his fingers, and chanted, "Forest of Burth, hear my spell. Grant me now a place to dwell."

A flash erupted, and a tall, thin tent appeared.

"That's amazing!" cheered Lucas. "But it's a little, um . . . little. How will you fit in there?"

Grom pulled back the flap. "Why don't you see for yourself?"

Lucas and Clara entered the tent.

The inside was huge and looked like the home of a nobleman. It had wood floors and real walls. There was a kitchen, a great room, a bedroom, and more. Ruskin flew to the top of the high ceiling and circled the great room.

"Not bad!" the prince exclaimed.

Clara turned around, taking it all in. "Nobody would ever guess this tiny tent could have such a magnificent home inside!"

Grom waved them off and slipped on his hiking boots.

"Now let's get to Goblin Falls before dark," Grom said, standing up and rubbing his hands together.

"Before dark? What happens after dark?" Lucas asked nervously.

"Um"—Grom paused awkwardly—"why, because we can't see the beauty of the falls in the dark, that's all."

Lucas and Clara looked at each other in surprise.

"I thought you said Goblin Falls was nothing special!" Lucas said.

Grom shrugged and said, "Don't try to figure me out. Wizards are mysterious. Now let's get going."

CHAPTER 2

Dire Howls

The forest trail was dark, except for the few shafts of sunlight that streamed through the trees. Lucas and Clara hopped over the spidery roots and moss-covered rocks to keep up with Grom. The wizard moved like a swift fox. His cloak fluttered behind him as he went down the trail.

Lucas wondered if Grom had something else on his mind.

The wizard wasn't acting like a happy hiker. His eyes were fixed on the trail, and his mouth was set in a thin, grim line. But Lucas pushed his concerns aside when he heard the thunderous roar of Goblin Falls in the distance.

"We're getting close!" Lucas called.

The rumble got louder and louder as the path led out of the forest and up onto a ridge. Grom reached the falls first, followed by the kids and Ruskin. They gaped at the rapids plunging over the cliff. The water seemed to vanish into the earth.

"Whoa!" cried Lucas. "It really *does* feel like you're on the edge of the world!"

Clara nodded and followed Lucas down the path beside the falls to get a better look.

Suddenly a sharp whistle rang out. The kids looked over at Grom.

He waved at them wildly. Lucas and Clara raced back up the path to his side.

"What's wrong?" asked Lucas.

Grom had gone white with fear. "Listen," he said.

Lucas and Clara heard a faint sound above the booming falls.

OW-OW-OWOOOOOO!

"It sounds like dogs howling," Lucas said.

Clara whispered, "Those aren't dogs. That's the cry of dire wolves."

Lucas could not believe it. "Impossible. Dire wolves only come out at night. Why would they howl during the day?"

More howls echoed, and Ruskin flew to Lucas.

He patted his dragon on the head. "Don't worry. The wolves won't bother us."

"Are you sure?" asked Clara. "My dad used to tell me lots of scary stories about dire wolves when I was younger."

"Lucas is right," Grom answered. "Those were made-up stories to scare little children. Dire wolves would never approach a human, because they don't trust them."

Then Grom marched back down the forest path. "We must return to the campsite."

Lucas and Clara could hear the concern in Grom's voice and moved to keep up with him. Ruskin also flew close behind.

The sun began to set, and the trail became harder to follow.

Darkness was everywhere, and the howling wolves turned the once-friendly forest creepy.

The kids and Grom hiked quickly, without a word, until they reached the campsite—and gasped.

The kids' tents had been torn and shredded to pieces.

"WHAT HAPPENED TO OUR TENTS?" cried Clara.

"And why is yours still standing, Grom?" Lucas noted.

Grom was busy. He was looking for danger in the dark edges of the camp.

"My tent has an invisibility charm. The attackers were unable to see it. But enough talk. We all need to get inside," he said.

The kids were frozen, staring at the damage.

"NOW," Grom commanded.

CHAPTER 3

Dire Lullaby

Lucas, Clara, and Ruskin all sat on pillows beside an enchanted blue fire. The magical flame was cool to the touch, yet still kept them warm.

Grom stood on the other side of the room, muttering a spell and tossing herbs into a simmering cauldron. The fumes began to shimmer and turned into a swirl of light that encircled the entire tent.

It was a protection spell.

"Do you think he'll use a spell to find the attackers too?" Clara asked.

Lucas took a marshmallow from the bag next to him and slid it onto a stick.

"No doubt," he said as he twirled the marshmallow over the blue flame.

Clara grabbed the bag away from Lucas. "How can you eat at a time like this?"

"We *are* camping, after all," said Lucas. "And it's not really camping until you eat melted marshmallows with troll chocolates."

Clara tried not to smile but couldn't resist.

The warm feeling didn't last long. Another dire wolf howl rang out in the distance. More howls answered back.

"Why are the dire wolves still howling?" Lucas asked Clara.

"I have no idea," she admitted, "but I know where we can find out."

Clara tossed a marshmallow to Ruskin, who happily ate it, and then she jumped up and pulled Lucas with her.

"Wait, my marshmallow!" whined Lucas, but it was too late. Ruskin ate it, too.

Without his sweet treat, Lucas trailed after Clara until they found a room filled with bookshelves.

"I was right!" said Clara. "Only a
wizard would bring a library on a
camping trip."

After searching for a book about dire wolves, the two friends sat down to learn more about the mysterious creatures.

"According to this, dire wolves are rarely seen by humans," Lucas said. "What we *do* know about dire wolves has been learned from studying their paw prints, abandoned dens, and, um . . . their wolf droppings."

There was a drawing of a paw print on the page. It was huge.

Clara took over. "It says dire wolves are as big as saber-toothed tigers! It also says they travel in packs and are fiercely loyal to their families."

They turned the page to study more drawings. The enormous wolves had thick, marbled fur coats and yellow eyes.

"They're beautiful," Clara said, yawning.

Lucas and Ruskin yawned too. Suddenly the long day of hiking caught up with them, and they were tired. They shuffled back to the great room and curled up on the pillows in front of the fire.

The sound of the howling wolves
lulled them to sleep.

CHAPTER 4

Dire Pup

Whap! Whap! Whap!

Lucas woke up to a flutter of dragon wings in his face. Ruskin was standing smack on the prince's chest. The little dragon hopped up and down excitedly and pointed his tail across the room.

Lucas heard an odd, high-pitched whimper and saw something moving in the shadows of the tent.

"What's going on?" Clara asked, rubbing her eyes.

"You're *not* going to believe this," Lucas whispered. "There's a dire wolf pup *inside with us.*"

Lucas and Clara watched the pup creep out from under the kitchen table. The pup's tail caught on the tablecloth, and she dragged it along with her. Plates, cups, and silverware crashed loudly to the floor.

The noise startled the pup and Ruskin. The dragon flew away, but the pup yelped and bounded over next to the kids.

Lucas carefully held out his hand, and the pup lifted her head to sniff it.

"It's okay," Lucas said softly. "You can trust me."

The wolf pup crawled into his lap, plumped down, and relaxed.

"You've got a new friend," said Clara.

Lucas watched the pup's chest lift and fall with every breath. "How did she get past Grom's spells?"

Clara thought for a moment. "Maybe the tent is open to anyone or anything that needs protection."

Lucas nodded. "Grom would definitely cast a spell like that."

Then the little wolf pup stood up and perked her ears. The children stopped talking and listened.

"Someone's talking outside," Lucas whispered. "It sounds like trolls."

Clara cupped a hand to her ear. "I hear humans, too."

The voices were close. So close, the kids froze.

"That pup has to be around here *somewhere!*" boomed a troll's gruff voice.

"Look at these torn tents," another troll said. "The pack is looking for the pup too."

Footsteps crunched closer to the wizard's tent. The kids held their breath even though they knew Grom's spell would protect them.

"We'd better find that pup first," one of the men said. "She would fetch us some big money."

Then they walked away from the campsite.

"They are *hunters!*" whispered Clara to Lucas.

Suddenly Grom stormed into the great room, and Lucas covered the wolf pup with a blanket without thinking.

"Did you hear that?!" Grom barked. He looked very angry. "Those fools are after a dire wolf, and that is against the law. You stay here. I'm going to find them and bring them to justice."

"Wait," said the prince, who wanted to tell Grom about the hidden pup.

But the wizard interrupted him. "I'm sorry, Prince Lucas, but this is too dangerous. You must stay here. And whatever you do, *do not* leave the tent. Your safety depends on it."

"Grom . . . ," started Clara.

The wizard pulled open the flap on the tent and looked over his shoulder.

"Don't worry, Clara. I've sent word to the king requesting help," he said. "Now do as I say and *stay put.*"

The flap slapped shut behind him,
and the kids were left alone . . . with
one sleepy dire pup.

CHAPTER 5

Dire Plan

Clara glared at the prince. "You know we should have told Grom about the pup."

Lucas grabbed his backpack and stuffed any food he could find into it: sausages, bread, fruit, and more.

"We tried," he said. "Besides, I have a plan."

"A plan?" Clara asked. "What kind of plan?"

Lucas smiled. "We're returning the pup to her wolf pack. Dire wolves travel every few days, so we don't have much time."

Clara nodded thoughtfully. "Good idea, but how is the pup going to follow us? *I'm* not putting her on a leash."

Lucas held up his bag of food. "You don't need a leash if you have snacks! Watch and learn."

The prince waved a sausage in front of the pup and walked around the tent. The pup sniffed the air, then followed Lucas everywhere. Ruskin was interested too.

Lucas tore the sausage into two pieces and tossed one to the pup and one to Ruskin. They both ate it up and looked back to Lucas, asking for more.

Lucas tossed another piece, and the pair collided trying to catch it.

The dire wolf pup let out a series of tiny sneezes.

"Looks like you are allergic to dragons, huh?" said Lucas. "We'll make sure to keep you two apart. Even a tiny dire wolf sneeze can be tracked by hunters."

As they stepped out of the tent, Lucas told Ruskin to fly overhead and look for signs of the wolf pack.

"Pay attention to caves, Ruskin," Lucas directed. "Wolves like to hide there during the day."

Ruskin squawked and took off.

The kids watched and waited for signals from Ruskin. Twice the dragon spied a cave, squawked, and  swooped down to check the cave for dire wolves. Both times, the dragon soared back into the sky and signaled *no*.

After checking a third cave, Ruskin didn't return.

"I wonder what's taking him so long?" Lucas said.

"Do you think he found the pack?" asked Clara.

A rumble of voices erupted from the forest. They were trolls . . . and they were cheering about a new catch.

"It's the *hunters*!" he cried. "They must have caught Ruskin!"

Clara grabbed Lucas by the arm. "We have to rescue him!"

Lucas picked up the pup and was about to run toward the shouting when a full-grown dire wolf stepped out of the forest. It snarled, and more snarls echoed around them.

Lucas and Clara were surrounded by the pack.

CHAPTER 6

Wolf Loyalty

The wolves bared their sharp teeth and growled. It was a message that Lucas heard loud and clear.

The prince quickly and carefully set the pup on the ground in front of the leader.

But the wolf pup turned around and ran *back* to Lucas. She sat on her hind legs, waiting for another treat.

Lucas and Clara didn't dare move. They wanted to be respectful to the wolves.

Soon a young wolf crept toward the wolf pup and nudged her. The pup barked playfully.

"Is that your pup?" Clara asked, daring to speak to the wolf.

The young wolf nodded as if he understood. The wolf's yellow eyes looked calm and mysterious.

"We mean no harm," Clara went on. "We wanted to return your pup safely."

The young wolf listened as he guided the pup back to the pack.

"Bad people were hunting your pup," Clara explained. "She hid in our tent."

Then Lucas spoke up. "Now the hunters have caught my friend—a scarlet dragon."

The leader of the pack stepped closer. "SILENCE!" he growled.

Lucas and Clara jumped back.

"You can *talk* . . . ?" Lucas said in amazement.

"Wolves can do a great many things," the leader said, "but we never run toward danger without a plan."

Lucas raised one eyebrow. "We *did* have a plan," he said. "We planned to return your pup and maybe spy on the hunters."

The wolf looked Lucas in the eye. "Spy on the hunters? We know all about the hunters," he said.

"They come by ship from another kingdom to capture Wrenly's creatures. They put them in cages and zip-line the cages over the bluffs to their ship. They do it for money. Now they want us."

Hearing this made Lucas very angry. He clenched his fists and asked, "Dire wolves, would you help us stop these awful hunters?"

The wolf narrowed his eyes. "Wolves only help *other* wolves," he said. "Today we spared your lives. Tomorrow we'll be gone."

Then the wolf turned and disappeared into the forest. The pack followed.

The little wolf pup raised her head and howled at Lucas and Clara. Then she trotted into the shadows and joined the others.

CHAPTER 7

Any Which Way

The kids raced through the dark forest to find Ruskin.

"Those wolves should've been *happy* we saved their pup," Lucas complained. "And they should've offered to help Ruskin too."

Clara hopped over a root. "I know how you feel," she said, "but dire wolves are only loyal to the pack, and we're not part of their pack."

Lucas didn't care about the ways of wolves. He just wanted to save his friend. He charged ahead in silence until they came to a clearing.

It was empty now, but there were wagon wheel prints on the dusty trail. Lucas also spotted scorch marks on the trees and could smell a hint of smoke in the air.

"The hunters captured Ruskin here," said the prince.

Clara touched one of the burnt tree trunks. It was still hot.

"Looks like Ruskin put up a good fight," she added. "Do you think he escaped?"

A branch snapped behind them, and Lucas and Clara spun around.

It was Grom, holding a bow loaded with an arrow. "Ruskin did *not* get away. The hunters trapped him. They used a powerful sleeping potion like this."

Grom lifted the arrow for the kids to see. Instead of an arrowhead on the end of the weapon, the arrow had a bag attached to it.

"This one bag could put an entire pack of dire wolves to sleep," the wizard told them. "I found it in the forest. It's how the hunters capture the creatures they've stolen."

With a wave of his hand, the wizard made the bow and arrow disappear. A scowl swept over his face. "Now tell me, Lucas and Clara, what part of 'stay put' did you not understand?"

Lucas drew a deep breath and explained what had happened. The old wizard sighed. He knew he couldn't keep the prince and Clara from helping solve the case of the hunters, especially now that Ruskin was involved.

"Okay," Grom said. "If we want to save Ruskin, then we'll have to move fast."

The team followed the wagon tracks through the forest, with Grom leading the way. The trail led to a clearing, where the one set of wagon tracks turned into several sets of tracks—all going in different directions.

"This must have been the hunters' meeting place," Grom said.

Lucas studied the crisscrossed wheel prints.

"They could've gone in any direction!" he exclaimed. "How do we know which one has Ruskin?"

Grom held his hands over the wagon tracks. "Let me handle this," he said before chanting a spell: "*Road, trail, or byway! Show us the right way!*"

Then he swooshed his hands across the air. Light flashed, followed by a clap of thunder.

Suddenly, Grom was trapped inside an enormous floating bubble. He pushed on the sides of the bubble, but he couldn't get free.

"The hunters set a counter curse!" he shouted. "They wanted to make sure no one could follow them. This magic even ejected their weapons. Look at the hunters' bow and arrow on the ground."

Lucas and Clara pounded against the bubble.

"It's no use," Grom said. "This is a timed spell. I'll be stuck here until the hunters escape."

Lucas kicked the dirt in front of him. "Now we'll *never* save Ruskin!"

Then a small howl pierced the night. Lucas and Clara both turned around. The dire wolf pup stood by the edge of the forest.

"Have you come to help?" Lucas asked.

The pup nodded and began to sniff the wagon wheel tracks until one set made her sneeze.

"She's done it!" Lucas cheered, remembering that the pup was allergic to dragons. "The sneeze means she's found Ruskin's scent!"

Grom rapped against the bubble. "Let the pup guide you! And take the bow and arrow for protection. Remember, the sleeping potion is powerful, but you'll only have one shot."

Clara nodded and picked up the bow and arrow. Then the kids and the pup followed the set of tracks.

"Hold on, Ruskin!" Lucas said under his breath. "We're coming!"

CHAPTER 8

On the Bluffs

Lucas and Clara followed the pup all the way to the Bluffs of Burth. Wagons with cages full of creatures were parked there.

The first cage held all kinds of birds: robins, barn owls, magpies, and cranes. The next cage had butterflies: yellow, orange, blue, and speckled. The cage after that held a drowsy grazzle bear.

And one cage had Ruskin, who was still asleep.

"Wow," Clara whispered. "This is a bigger rescue mission than we thought."

Lucas nodded. "Look, there's the zip line going over the side of the bluff. I wonder why the creatures haven't been lowered onto the ship?"

Clara nudged Lucas and pointed toward the hunters, who were sitting on the rocks eating a meal. The hunters had their backs to the children, who counted four trolls and two humans.

"They are eating a meal first," Clara said.

"Perfect. Let's free the creatures before they finish," Lucas said. "You get the butterflies and birds. I'll get Ruskin and the other animals."

Then they crept toward the cages.

When Lucas reached Ruskin's cage, he heard a tiny sneeze behind him. The dire wolf pup had followed him, and the pup was allergic to dragons!

"ACHOO!" the pup sneezed.

Then everything happened at once: Ruskin woke up and screeched.

Clara freed the butterflies and birds,
and they flapped into the sky. And
the hunters dropped their food and
ran to save their animal prizes.

"Nab the dire wolf FIRST!" cried
one of the hunters. "Then grab those
kids!"

The rescue mission was doomed.

CHAPTER 9

Power of the Pack

One of the hunters lunged for the pup and scooped her into his arms.

At the same time, Clara raised her bow, loaded the sleeping potion arrow, and pointed it at the hunter.

"Drop the pup!" she ordered. "Or I'll put you all to sleep!"

The hunter slowed down and snapped his fingers. The rest of the hunters surrounded the kids.

"Okay, playtime is over, so put down your arrow," the hunter said. "We have a job to finish, and it looks like you're outnumbered. Oh, and let me remind you, it's a long way down to those monster-infested waters."

Lucas didn't budge. "She *said* drop the wolf pup. NOW."

The hunter shrugged. "Okay, have it your way."

Suddenly a tiny sneeze erupted from the wolf pup . . . right in the hunter's face. Slobber and snot were everywhere!

"YUCK!" yelled the hunter as he dropped the pup.

She scampered over to Lucas and stood in front of him, growling fiercely at the trolls and men.

The wispy growl only made the hunters laugh.

"Is your baby wolf going to save you now?" one of the trolls chuckled. "I doubt it. Hey, guys, I think these kids need a little nap."

The hunters pulled back their loaded bows, but they never had time to shoot.

The dire wolf pack thundered onto the bluff and surrounded the hunters, who dropped their arrows.

The sleeping potions struck their
feet and burst open.

Instantly, the hunters dropped to
the ground and began to snore.

Lucas wasted no time. He ran
to the cages and freed Ruskin and
the trapped animals. They were
still groggy from the sleeping potion.
Lucas hugged his dragon.

Then he looked over the bluff and saw several ships surrounding the hunters' ship.

"It's the Wrenly royal fleet!" he yelled to Clara. "They've caught the hunters!"

Clara had just set the bow and arrow down in front of the dire wolf pack leader. She bowed and stepped back. The dire wolves bowed too.

"You and the prince have proven you are friends to the animals," the leader said. "Please come back to our den so we may honor you with a gift."

CHAPTER 10

Wolf Family Friends

First the children signaled to the royal fleet to let them know where they were. Then they tied the hands and feet of the sleeping hunters. The king would deal with them now.

Lucas turned to the wolves. "We only have a little time before we have to leave," he said.

The pack leader nodded and said, "Follow us."

The wolves led Lucas and Clara to a cave in the forest where the night still covered the land. Inside, there was a wide-open space with dark passages that led to many different chambers. The moonlight sparkled off the rock walls, which made the room glow.

"This is amazing," Clara gasped.

Lucas nodded as he watched the wolves gather around their leader.

Then the leader spoke.

"Our pack would like to honor both of you. You risked your lives for your dragon and for the innocent animals of Wrenly. You stood up to the evil hunters. You also cared for our pup when she was separated from the pack, and you had the courage to bring her back to us. Prince Lucas and Lady Clara, you have won the trust of the dire wolves. It is our honor to invite you to be members of our pack. Do you accept our offer?"

Lucas looked at Clara, and then they both turned back to the leader.

"Yes, we accept this great honor!" the prince declared.

Then the wolves began to howl in harmony. It wasn't the eerie wail they had heard in the forest. It sounded like a beautiful song. As they listened, the kids understood the howl. The wolves were singing, *"Welcome, wolf family friends."*

The two best friends felt a new power surround them like a force field. It was the power of being part of a pack. Lucas and Clara would always look out for the animals of Wrenly. And now the dire wolves would always look out for them.

Enter

The Kingdom of Wrenly